DRAGON SLAYERS' ACADEMY™ 11

DANGER!
WIZARD AT WORK

By Kate McMullan

Illustrated by Bill Basso

GROSSET & DUNLAP • NEW YORK

To the Three Amigos—Scott Onnink, Jimmy Sarafin
and Kevin TenDolle, and to their gifted
teacher, Ms. Mary Jo Balde—K. McM.

For Harris, one brave dragon slayer—B.B.

Text copyright © 2004 by Kate McMullan. Illustrations copyright © 2004 by Bill Basso.
All rights reserved. Published by Grosset & Dunlap, a division of Penguin Young Readers
Group, 345 Hudson Street, New York, New York 10014. GROSSET & DUNLAP is a
trademark of Penguin Group (USA) Inc. Printed in the U.S.A.

Library of Congress Cataloging-in-Publication Data

McMullan, Kate.
  Danger! wizard at work / by Kate McMullan ; illustrated by Bill Basso.
    p. cm.–(Dragon Slayers' Academy ; 11)
  Summary: When a wizard's spell goes awry and turns Wiglaf and his friends, Angus
and Eric, into dragons, they spend a few days at Dragon Slackers Academy—a school for
dragons with bad attitudes.
  ISBN 0-448-43529-2 (pbk.)
  [1. Wizards—Fiction. 2. Dragons—Fiction. 3. Schools—Fiction.] I. Basso, Bill, ill. II. Title.
  PZ7.M2295Dan 2004
  [Fic]–dc22   2003023597

ISBN 0-448-43529-2   10 9 8 7 6 5 4 3 2 1

Chapter 1

"Up and at 'em, dragon slayers!" called Frypot, the DSA school cook.

Wiglaf opened an eye. It wasn't light out yet. He closed it again. Maybe he was dreaming.

"Up, I say! It's a beautiful day at DSA!" Frypot banged a pot lid with his soup ladle. CLANG! CLANG! CLANG!

Wiglaf jumped up. All the Class I lads did. They knew Frypot would keep banging until they were on their feet.

"What's for breakfast, Frypot?" called Angus.

"Eggs and bacon, lads," said Frypot. "All you can eat."

Eggs and bacon? Wiglaf couldn't believe it. Frypot never fed them anything but scrambled eel.

"Eel eggs, Frypot?" called Erica, who was a princess but disguised herself as a boy so she could go to all-boys DSA. Wiglaf and Angus were the only lads who knew her secret.

"Nah," said Frypot. "They're the real thing. Found 'em in the cupboard this morning."

"Hooray!" cheered Class I.

"I'm going to be first in line!" Angus yanked on his DSA tunic.

"I'll be second," said Erica, racing for the door. "Hurry up, Wiggie. Let's go!"

Wiglaf dressed quickly. The three friends headed for the cafeteria with throngs of other DSA students.

As they ran by the headmaster's office, Mordred stuck his head out.

"Egad! A stampede!" he cried.

Mordred spied Angus. "Not so fast,

nephew!" he called. "I need a word with you."

"Uncle...no!" Angus panted, already short of breath. "Got to get...to the caf...eteria!"

"Now!" Mordred grabbed him. "Eric and Wiglaf, you come, too. This is a three-lad job."

Wiglaf sighed. Mordred's jobs always had a way of turning out badly—for Wiglaf. The DSA headmaster picked on Wiglaf more than any other student. Was it because he was small for his age? Because he had carrot-colored hair? By rights, Mordred should like him best of all, for Wiglaf had slain two dragons—one named Gorzil and then Gorzil's mother, who had come to seek revenge. True, Wiglaf had killed them both by accident. He would never kill any creature on purpose. In fact, he and Angus had "adopted" a baby dragon. They called him Worm and kept him hidden in the library, safe from the headmaster.

"Oh, Mordred, sir!" Erica cried. "Can we not come see you after breakfast?"

"Pretty please, with a great big pile of gold coins on top?" begged Angus.

"Missing breakfast won't kill you," Mordred boomed as he herded the three students into his office. "Here, look at the latest issue of *Greed*." He waved a scroll in their faces, then rolled it down so the three could read for themselves.

SPECIAL OFFER—THIS WEEK ONLY!
Hermit Harry's Jiffy-Gold™ Alchemy Kit
GUARANTEED to turn worthless household
items into solid GOLD household items
worth a bloody fortune!
Pick up your FREE Jiffy-Gold™ today!
Take it home and try Jiffy-Gold™ for a week.
If not completely satisfied, return the Jiffy-
Gold™ no payment due, no questions asked.
"Hermit Harry—he may stink,
but his prices don't!"
Just follow your nose to Hermit Harry's Hut—
Dark Forest, south of Nowhere Swamp.

Wiglaf and his pet pig, Daisy, had hiked through Nowhere Swamp on their way to DSA. It was there, in Wizard's Bog, that they'd met Zelnoc, a mixed-up wizard. He'd put a speech spell on Daisy. Now she could talk—but only in pig Latin.

"I want that kit today!" Mordred boomed. "Why, in a week, I can Jiffy-Gold the whole castle. Then I'll return the kit and I won't have to pay a penny. Oh, it's too good to pass up."

"Mother always says if something sounds too good to be true, it probably is," said Angus.

"What does she know?" grumbled Mordred. "Off with you to Hermit Harry's. Be gone! Get me that Jiffy-Gold!"

"Nowhere Swamp is a day's walk from here, sir," Wiglaf pointed out. "We shall have to spend the night in the scary Dark Forest."

"So?" said Mordred. "Get going!"

"Yes, Uncle," said Angus. "Right after breakfast. It's bacon and eggs this morning."

"I don't care what you eat!" cried Mordred. "Just go! Just—" The DSA headmaster paused. "Blazing King Ken's britches!" he cried, his oversized violet eyes widening in horror. "Frypot is feeding the lads *my* eggs and bacon! They're *mine*!"

Mordred ran out of his office, his red cape billowing out behind him. "Oh, if that cook is feeding my eggs and bacon to students, I'll put him in thumbscrews!" Mordred turned, and glared at Wiglaf, Angus, and Erica, who were standing at his office door. "What are you waiting for?" he growled at them. "Get me that Jiffy-Gold! I want it here tomorrow, or I'll put you all in thumbscrews! Go, go, GO!"

The three took off running down the hallway.

"I'm soooo hungry!" Angus said when they reached the Class I dorm.

"There's always your stash," Wiglaf pointed out.

Angus shot Wiglaf a look. Angus was famous at DSA for the amazing goodie boxes his mother sent him. He hardly ever shared. But now he filled a large bag with gummy worms, jelly beans, chocolate spiders, and marshmallows.

The three packed what little else they needed for the trip. From inside Mordred's office, they heard the headmaster sobbing, "Oh, my eggs and bacon—wasted on boys!"

Before they left the castle yard, the boys made a quick trip to the library. Wiglaf wanted to be sure Worm had enough food. He told the young dragon to be good while they were away. Then he stopped at the henhouse to say good-bye to his pet pig.

When Daisy heard that they were going into the Dark Forest, she said, "E-bay areful-cay!"

"We shall be careful, Daisy," Wiglaf promised.

All morning, the three friends trudged on.

They kept Swamp River on their right. Even in the daytime, the Dark Forest was dark. Owls hooted. Bats screeched. Then, under the other forest sounds, Wiglaf heard a low growl.

It grew louder.

"Do you hear something?" Wiglaf asked.

"I-I think so," said Erica. She did not sound like her usual brave self.

Now the growler let rip with a terrible, blood-chilling roar.

Wiglaf, Angus, and Erica shrieked. They clung together in a frozen clump.

"A wild animal!" cried Angus. "We're doomed! We're doomed!"

Chapter 2

oads and toadstools!" shouted a voice.

Wiglaf knew that voice. "Zelnoc?" he called. "Is that you?"

A white-bearded face topped by a pointed hat appeared high in the branches of a gnarly tree.

"Could be," he said. "Who wants to know?"

"Wiglaf," said Wiglaf.

"You again!" cried Zelnoc. The wizard floated down toward the DSA students. His star-speckled robe fluttered in the breeze. "How was my roar?"

"Loud," said Erica.

"Scary," said Angus.

"Ah, good." Zelnoc smiled. "Roaring is wonderful for a wizard's soul. Makes us feel powerful." His face fell. "And I could use some extra power. I'm in a bit of a pickle." He skidded to a halt in front of them, pinwheeling his arms to keep from losing his balance.

The wizard didn't look so good. Wiglaf saw that he had dark circles under his eyes, as if he hadn't slept in weeks.

"Zelnoc, what's wrong?" asked Wiglaf.

Zelnoc sighed. "Oh, a little spell went wrong. Nothing I can't undo, given time. And a really, really powerful spell-reversal spell."

"What spell went wrong, wizard?" asked Erica.

"The Young Again spell," said Zelnoc. "Zizmor's been working on it for ages. I happened to see his notes lying around his tower the other night. I started messing around, making improvements. When Ziz came in, okay, maybe I shouldn't have tried it out on him. But I wanted to impress him. He is my boss." Zelnoc shook his head. "Now I've got to do a spell-reversal spell. That's the trickiest kind! But if I don't do it—and soon!—the Wizards' Committee will take away my wand!"

Wiglaf's heart went out to the troubled wizard. Zelnoc always tried to help when Wiglaf summoned him.

"We need a spell, Zelnoc," said Wiglaf. "I'll bet you can help us."

Erica elbowed him. "Wiggie!" she whispered. "You must be jesting. A spell from Zelnoc is the last thing we need."

"We need to get to Hermit Harry's Hut," Wiglaf pointed out.

"Do you know where that is, wizard?" asked Angus.

"Doesn't everyone?" Zelnoc pinched his nose as though something smelled really, really bad.

"We know it's south of Nowhere Swamp,"

said Wiglaf. "But that's all we know."

"You don't need a spell." Zelnoc sighed. "You need directions. Head south. If you cut through Nowhere Swamp, it'll take a day off your journey. But watch out for the quicksand. And the crocs. They're very hungry this time of year."

Wiglaf swallowed. "Crocodiles?"

Zelnoc nodded. "If you come out of the swamp alive, walk south to where two roads meet. You'll come upon the Crone of the Crossroads. If she's in a bad mood, that's the end of your journey. Buh-bye! But if you make it by her, veer left, past the graveyard—I don't recommend cutting through *that*—you'll come to the Tower of Mysterious Light. There, take a right—"

"Wizard, stop!" cried Angus. "Please! Put a get-there-quick spell on us. Can you?"

"Do warlocks have warts?" replied the wizard. "Do damsels have distress?"

"Oh, do it!" said Angus. "I don't want to spend the night in the Dark Forest."

Erica folded her arms. "No need. We can get there ourselves."

"Off you go, then," Zelnoc said. "Oh, and keep to the path. Fewer poisonous snapping turtles there."

Erica sighed. "You win, wizard. Do your spell. But it better work."

"Worry not!" cried the wizard. "You're going to like this one." Zelnoc pushed up the sleeves of his wizard robe. "They're going to beg me to speak at the next Wizards' Convention after they get a load of this spell. Close your eyes, kiddos. Here we go."

Wiglaf closed his eyes. He heard Zelnoc singing:

> *"Flies have 'em,*
> *Bees have 'em,*
> *Even itchy little fleas have 'em.*

Now, presto! You'll have 'em, too.
Ring-a-ding-a—wings!"

As Zelnoc sang, Wiglaf felt his shoulder blades growing. He heard a ripping sound. Was that his DSA tunic? He began to feel dizzy.

Zelnoc sang on:

> *"Ducks have 'em,*
> *Hens have 'em,*
> *Even funny little penguins have 'em.*
> *Now, presto! You'll have 'em, too.*
> *Ring-a-ding-a—wings!"*

Wings were sprouting out of Wiglaf's back! He was sure of it. He opened one eye just a crack and saw Zelnoc twirling as he belted out:

> *"Vampire bats in their caves have 'em,*
> *Scaly dragons do, too.*

Wings, baby, you've got 'em,
Oh, what Zelnoc can do!"

"Wizard!" cried Angus. "Stop!"

Suddenly, a terrible dizziness overtook Wiglaf. His head whirled. He felt sick. He felt his whole body growing. RRIPPPPP! He felt as if he was bursting through his skin. He felt his neck growing longer. Teeth pushed up out of his gums. His eyeballs felt like inflating balloons. And what was that growing out of his backside? Dizziness took over. Wiglaf felt as if he was falling, falling.

Then all was quiet.

Wiglaf opened his eyes. He glanced over his shoulder at his back. Yep, he had wings. Not feathery little birdie wings, either. Huge, silvery, scaled wings.

"Angus?" he called. "Erica?"

No answer.

Wiglaf looked around. Everything was a

blur. He blinked. He thought he saw Angus and Erica. But, no. Those weren't his friends. He blinked again. Now he saw that standing where Angus and Erica had been were two dragons!

Chapter 3

Wiglaf stared at the dragons. One was silver. The other was blue. They weren't very big.

Wiglaf looked down at his arms. Green. Scaly. His hands were green and scaly. He had claws!

"Ahhhh!" he screamed. "We're dragons!"

Zelnoc snorted. "Okay, okay. But you've got wings, haven't you? Wings will get you where you want to go—and fast! I meant to give you dragon wings so you could fly to Hermit Harry's. Guess my spell is a little bit more powerful than I thought." He shrugged.

"Turn us back into us," said Erica.

"That would take a spell-reversal spell," said Zelnoc. "Oh, sure, I could sing the whole song backwards. That would do it. But the chances of me tripping up are astronomical. Then who knows what you might turn into? No, best to stay dragons until I figure out my reversal."

"When will that be?" asked Wiglaf.

Zelnoc looked thoughtful. "Under a year, I'd say."

"A year!" cried all three dragons.

"Maybe sooner," Zelnoc said. "Or the spell might wear off on its own. Who knows? Not me. I'd best go back to my tower. Transform some toads. Mutate some mice. That sort of thing. See what I can figure out. I'll be back. Tah-tah!"

A cloud of blue smoke billowed from out of nowhere and swallowed up the wizard.

The silver dragon glared at Wiglaf.

"You think this is my fault, don't you?" Wiglaf said.

Erica folded her spindly forearms and said nothing.

Angus, meanwhile, was studying what he could see of himself. "Hey, I know I'm blue and I've got a big white belly. But what does my face look like?"

Wiglaf was happy for a change of subject. "You have a mouth full of pointy teeth," he told Angus. "A long snout. Blue eyes with yellow centers. And two stubby white horns on your head."

"How about me?" asked Erica.

"Your face is shiny silver, like the rest of you," Wiglaf told her. "You have green eyes, a curved horn on your snout, and a matching one on top of your head."

"Cool," said Erica.

"What about me?" said Wiglaf.

"Green face," Angus told him. "Yellow eyes with black triangles in the middle. And a bright red crest on top of your head. Hey, it just started blinking!"

Wiglaf smiled. It sounded as if he was a very good-looking dragon. He wished Worm was here to see him. "At least now we can fly to Hermit Harry's to get the Jiffy-Gold," he pointed out.

"Do you really think we can fly?" asked Angus.

"Let's find out," said Erica.

Using muscles he never knew he had, Wiglaf unfurled a pair of great wings. Angus and Erica did, too. They began flapping and...

Up they went.

Wiglaf was just getting the hang of flying when a silvery streak whizzed by him. Was that Erica? He turned to see. Big mistake! He felt himself tilting, falling. He flapped harder. Which way was up? No way to tell. He crash-landed in some bushes.

"Ow!" he said. He felt his crest. He hoped it wasn't bent.

He heard another crash. He looked up to see Erica perching unsteadily in the gnarly tree.

"Hey! Look up here!" called Angus.

Wiglaf saw a bright blue dragon circling easily overhead.

"Flying is great!" Angus called. "I love it!"

Angus landed. He gave Erica and Wiglaf a few pointers. Soon all three were soaring high above the Dark Forest. What a great feeling, gliding on the wind! No wonder Worm liked to sneak out of the library and fly around DSA. There was only one thing that worried Wiglaf.

"What if the spell wears off while we're up here?" he called to the others.

"Good point," said Erica. "Let's fly to Hermit Harry's as fast as we can." She surveyed the ground below. "I think it's that way. Follow me!"

Silver dragon in the lead, the three flew over the Dark Forest. A full moon lit the sky.

They flew over hills and valleys dotted with small villages. The hills below grew bigger. Zelnoc hadn't said anything about mountains! Where were they? Wiglaf's muscles began to ache. Flying was fun, but hard work. He needed a rest.

"Let's take a break," Wiglaf called.

"Hug your wings close to your body and you'll zoom down fast!" called Angus.

The three landed on a rocky peak.

"What's *that?*" Wiglaf squinted through the dark. Down in the valley, he saw what looked like a huge stone building. He was pretty sure it wasn't Hermit Harry's Hut.

"Let's take a closer look," suggested Angus.

They flew down to a riverbank. The river, wide and swift, shimmered in the moonlight. On an island in the middle of the river stood a great walled castle.

"Look," said Angus. He pointed a claw toward a sign on the castle wall.

When Wiglaf read what it said, his crest began blinking on and off.

"It says DSA!" Wiglaf couldn't believe his black-and-yellow eyes.

"Has Uncle Mordred opened another school?" Angus wondered out loud.

Once more, Wiglaf heard a noise. "Do you hear growling?" he asked.

"Take it easy," said Angus. "It's just my stomach."

"I'm hungry, too," said Erica. "Let's see what's left in your stash, Angus."

"Oh, rats! I left it behind," Angus said. "Let's go into that DSA and get something to eat. Then we can figure out what to do."

"We can't!" said Wiglaf. "DSA is a school for dragon *slayers*. And we're dragons!"

"Hmm," said Angus. "Could be dangerous. But I'm really hungry!"

"I know," said Erica. "Let's sneak into the castle while it's still dark and raid the kitchen."

They had a plan. Angus spread his wings. He glided over the river, up and over the wall, landing in the castle yard. Wiglaf and Erica followed.

This yard was much bigger than their own DSA castle yard. The three dragons made their way across it. Wiglaf wasn't used to walking on dragon feet. He felt awkward, off balance, as if his body was too heavy for his legs. But on he lumbered.

Erica slowly opened the castle door. They tiptoed inside. No one was around. In the dim light, they made their way down the hallway and up a set of stairs, hoping the kitchen was in the same spot as the kitchen at their own DSA.

Angus stuck his head in a door. "Here it is!" he whispered. Erica and Wiglaf hurried in after him.

The kitchen was lit by a narrow shaft of soft pre-dawn light.

"We have to hurry," Angus said, opening the pantry. "They'll be up soon. There's a ton of spaghetti in here. Wait. It's not spaghetti. It's dried eel grass!"

Wiglaf found a jar. Its label said *Eel Slime Sauce*. Yuck!

"Ew!" exclaimed Erica. "Jars of pickled eel. All this stuff looks disgusting!"

"Excuse me?" a voice boomed out from behind them.

Wiglaf looked up. His crest began blinking at triple speed.

Standing in the kitchen doorway was a very big, very red dragon.

Chapter 4

"Blazing britches!" Angus squeaked.

"Whoa," said Erica.

Wiglaf couldn't have spoken if his life depended on it. He just kept blinking.

The dragon was twice their size. Violet tentacles sprouted from the top of his scaly red skull. He wore a rumpled cook's apron.

"Looking for something?" the dragon asked, narrowing his beady orange eyes.

"F-f-f-food," Angus managed.

The big dragon blew twin smoke rings from two holes on the sides of his head. "No eating between meals at DSA."

"But we're hungry," said Angus.

"You'll wait for breakfast like the others," said the cook. "You must be new students."

Wiglaf felt as if his whole head was blinking. New students? Was this DSA a school for *dragons*?

"I am Sizzlegizzard," said the dragon, hissing white smoke as he spoke. "School cook." He walked over to a cupboard. He took out a skillet and a jar. He opened the jar and poured what looked like green spaghetti into the skillet. Then he took a breath and blew out a jet of orange flame, setting the spaghetti aflame. "DSA is a last-chance school for dragons who have been kicked out of all the decent dragon schools. You know that, don't you?"

Wiglaf shook his head in time with his wildly blinking crest.

"Yes, here at DSA we work with the worst of the worst!" Sizzlegizzard jiggled the skillet as he spoke. "If you get booted out of DSA, there's nowhere to go. End of the line. So we have rules here to shape up young slackers like you. Lots of rules." He flipped the contents of the skillet and bent down to flame it again. "If you don't follow the rules, you'll be sent to Madam Dragonova." As he spoke her name, the violet tendrils on the top of his head began to quiver. "And you don't want that."

Wiglaf, Erica, and Angus pressed close together. They were quivering, too. Even Erica.

"You know, Sizzlegizzard," Angus said, "I think we've come to the wrong school."

"Yes!" said Wiglaf eagerly. "It's all a mistake."

"Bye!" said Erica. "Nice meeting you!"

The three turned and raced for the kitchen door. But when they opened it, they found themselves face to face with a huge dragon. This one was twice Sizzlegizzard's size, and covered snout to claw with dull gray scales. He stared at the little dragons with cold, half-lidded gray eyes.

"Oh, it's you, Drigon," said Sizzlegizzard. "More new students. Take them down to the Class I dorm, will you?"

With a nod, Drigon herded the three new dragon students out of the kitchen and down the hallway. When they reached an arched doorway, Drigon shoved Wiglaf, Angus, and Erica into a dark room. It smelled nasty, as if something had been left smoldering on the stove. A chorus of snores and snorts filled the air. By the glow of his crest, Wiglaf was able to make out dozens of mounds on the floor. Each mound was a sleeping dragon.

Poking them with a claw, Drigon herded them to the back of the room, where they found unoccupied piles of rags. The three quickly dove for the piles. Dragon beds, Wiglaf guessed. Drigon fixed them with a dark gray stare.

Wiglaf shut his eyes. His heart was racing. He hardly knew what to think. One minute,

he and his friends had been on an errand for their greedy headmaster. The next minute, they'd been turned into dragons and plunked down inside a school for problem dragons. He feared to open his eyes. He didn't want to see Drigon hulking over him. In a short time, he fell asleep.

"Up and at 'em!" called a voice. "Up, I say! It's a beautiful day at DSA!" BANG! BANG! BANG!

Frypot! Wiglaf smiled sleepily. The whole thing had been a bad dream. He yawned and stretched. He sat up just as a plump blue dragon rolled out of bed and bumped into him.

This was no dream.

BANG! BANG! BANG! Sizzlegizzard was banging on a skillet with a meat cleaver.

Wiglaf stretched his dragon's body. He felt stiff from sleeping on the rags. He stood up and looked around. None of the other dragons had rolled out of bed. Most were still snoring, with their long pink tongues lolling out of their mouths.

"Don't make me call Drigon," Sizzlegizzard said.

Every dragon in the room leaped up. They didn't bother smoothing their tendrils, straightening their crests or horns, dusting off their scales, or brushing their fangs. They quickly put on their blue uniforms with gold letters spelling out DSA.

Wiglaf saw a folded uniform beside his rag pile. He didn't want to stick out, so he put it on. Erica and Angus did the same.

"We have to get out of here," whispered Erica. "And fast!"

"Not that fast," said Angus. "We're staying for breakfast."

"Are you crazy?" hissed Erica.

But before she could say another word, a green-and-white striped dragon with sleepy brown eyes hopped over to them. Her tendrils were tied in two pigtails.

"Peace, guys," she said. "I'm Sissy. Who are you?"

"I'm, uh, I'm Silvershine," said Erica, taking her name from her scales.

"Zoomer," said Angus. "You should see me fly."

Wiglaf had not given any thought to a dragon name. His crest was his most unusual feature. Maybe he could find a name in that.

"I'm Blinky," Wiglaf said. He was instantly sorry. Blinky sounded like someone's parakeet.

"So, what school did you guys get kicked out of?" asked Sissy.

"Oh, it's so small, you probably never heard of it," said Erica. "How about you?"

"Knightshredder Prep," said Sissy. "I got caught not smoking in the girls' bathroom. Plus, I made friends with the villagers I was supposed to eat." She shrugged. "So here I am at Dragon Slackers' Academy."

So that's what DSA stands for, thought Wiglaf.

"Bummer," said Erica. "How do you like it here?"

"It's awful!" said Sissy. "The teachers here are really mean. They're always making us burn things up." She shuddered. "You guys won't believe how much homework they pile on. Tons!"

"How's the food?" asked Angus.

"Oh, it's great," said Sissy.

Angus's blue eyes lit up.

"But only if you guys happen to like moat weedghetti with moat slime sauce," Sissy added. "Which I do not. Come on, I'll take you to the cafeteria. But I'm warning you guys—don't get your hopes up."

Chapter 5

he Dragon Slackers' Academy cafeteria looked just like the one back at DSA. Except that it was ten times bigger and filled with fire-breathing dragons.

"I hope Zelnoc's spell doesn't wear off now," Erica whispered as they lined up.

"We'd be toast," said Angus, picking up a cafeteria tray.

Wiglaf's crest began blinking at the thought. He picked up a tray, too.

"Raw eel?" wailed Angus as Sizzlegizzard plopped some onto his plate.

The dragon cook fixed him with an orange glare. "Are you complaining?"

"No, no, no, no, no," said Angus.

Wiglaf and Erica got their eel and hurried after Sissy and Angus to the Class I table.

"This is Zoomer, Stickley," Sissy was telling a small, sand-colored dragon with a prickly purple crest. "That's Silvershine and that's Blinky."

Stickley nodded. Then he picked up a raw eel from his plate. He tossed it into the air and breathed out a blast of fire—WHOOSH! The eel cooked in the air. Stickley caught it and gulped it down.

"Wow!" exclaimed Angus. "How did you *do* that?"

"You guys didn't have to cook your own food at your old school, I guess," said Sissy. "Me, neither. We had a chef at Knightshredder. Great food!" She sighed, cooking all the eels on her plate at once.

"I have to try this." Angus took a breath, tossed an eel into the air, and blew on it with all his might. But the raw eel splatted back onto his plate.

Erica had no better luck than Angus.

Then Wiglaf picked up an eel. He held it in front of his mouth and blew. WHOOSH! He was so surprised when he breathed out fire that he dropped the flaming eel.

"Whoa!" said Angus. "Tell me how to do it!"

"Try curling your tongue." Wiglaf stuck his tongue out to show them. Then he picked up the eel and popped it into his mouth. He didn't like eel much, but this one tasted pretty good.

As he ate, something hit Wiglaf on the back of his head. SPLAT!

"Sorry and peace, dude!" called a yellow-and-black dragon from the next table. He had a shiny black crest. "I was aiming for Sissy." He tried again. This time, he hit his mark.

"Thanks, Taxi!" cried Sissy. "Here, have some of mine!" She hurled some eel at him.

"Food fight! Food fight!" called the other dragons.

"It's just like DSA," said Wiglaf, ducking as a wad of eel sailed over the Class I table.

"Not exactly," said Angus.

Wiglaf saw what Angus meant. Now flaming spitballs were whizzing across the cafeteria. A chair caught on fire.

A cry went up: "Douser! Douser!"

A plump blue-green dragon galumphed over to the burning chair. He drew a breath and— WHOOSH! Instead of flames, water spurted out of his mouth, quickly putting out the fire.

All the dragons began to clap and cheer: "Nice one, Douser! Way to go, Douser!"

"At my old school, we had fire extinguishers," said Sissy. "Here, they make the students do everything."

Just then, Wiglaf caught sight of a large green dragon with many double chins. She stood on a platform at the front of the room. A rolled-up scroll of *Hoard* magazine stuck out from the pocket of her long red cloak. She gazed out at the students with large violet eyes.

"Greetings, slackers!" she barked.

"Greetings, Madam Dragonova!" the dragon students singsonged.

"Who's got gold for me today?" asked the DSA headmistress.

No one raised a claw.

"So no one has robbed or plundered to get me gold for my hoard?" she asked.

"No, Madam Dragonova," replied the dragon students in one voice.

"And I don't suppose any of you have stolen a dragon slayer's golden hoard?" she asked.

"No, Madam Dragonova," came the chorus.

"Listen up, slackers," Madam Dragonova growled. "You lily-livered lizards have been kicked out of some of the finest dragon schools in the world. Now you're at Dragon Slackers'

Academy. This is as low as you go. The bottom of the barrel. The pit."

Some dragon students hung their scaly heads. Wiglaf felt sorry for them.

"Here at DSA, we will make real dragons out of you!" Madam said. "We will teach you how to flame—and I'm not talking flaming spitballs here. I'm talking burning down whole villages!"

Some of the dragon students groaned.

Madam Dragonova ignored them. "We will teach you how to torch knights. How to rampage. How to plunder. How to destroy the countryside. How to root out dragon slayers and DO THEM IN!"

Many of the dragon students put their heads down on the tables. They didn't look one bit interested in doing any stuff like that.

Madam Dragonova's plum-colored eyes came to rest on Wiglaf, Angus, and Erica.

"Ah, Sizzlegizzard said we had new

students," she said. "Stand and say what brought you to Dragon Slackers' Academy." She aimed a claw at Wiglaf. "You first."

Wiglaf's crest blinked as he rose. "I'm, uh, Blinky," he managed. "I got sent here because...I can't stand the sight of blood," he added truthfully. He sat down.

Madam D. frowned. She stroked her chins with a withered claw. "Coach Blazer teaches our Blood, Gore, and Guts Class. I'll get him to give you a private lesson."

Wiglaf hoped that Zelnoc would get them out of there before he had to sit through *that*.

Madam pointed at Angus. The blue dragon stood. "I'm Zoomer," he said. "And I got kicked out of my old school for eating marshmallows in class."

"Way to go, dude!" called Taxi. Many of the students clapped for Angus.

"Marshmallows?" Madam looked disgusted. "Real dragons eat Red Hots."

Erica stood up. "The name's Silvershine," she said. "I got kicked out of my old school for being friends with a dragon slayer."

"You three are the worst dragons ever to set claw in DSA!" cried the headmistress. "You won't like it, but I'm going to make real dragons out of you, or my name isn't Ivana Dragonova."

Chapter 6

fter lunch, the three worst dragons ever to set claw in Dragon Slackers' Academy sneaked away. They hid in an empty room on the second floor of the castle.

"Conlez! Conlez! Conlez!" Wiglaf chanted. Saying the wizard's name backwards was the way to summon Zelnoc.

But no wizard appeared.

Wiglaf shrugged. "Maybe he's turned off his summoner. He does that when he takes a bath."

Wiglaf was just about to give it another try when a big green dragon stuck his head in at the door. "Thought I heard voices in here," he said. He had blue eyes that matched his blue blazer. He wore a hat with a brim. A silver whistle hung from a chain around his neck. "You're the new slackers."

The three nodded.

"I'm Coach Blazer." He checked his clipboard. "Outside with you now. Or you'll be late for my Taking Care of Dragon Slayers Class."

In the yard, Wiglaf saw Sissy, Stickley, Taxi, and Douser waiting with a mob of other young dragons. Nearby was a scarecrow. It looked like a knight with a wooden sword tied to one arm.

"Today, I will show you what to do if a dragon slayer is stalking you," said Coach. "Stickley! Demonstrate the Whirl and Flame."

"Aw, Coach!" whined Stickley. "Do I have to?"

"Stop stalling," said Coach Blazer. "Run over to old Straw Guts and show us."

"That scarecrow is a practice knight!" Wiglaf whispered to Angus and Erica. "Just like our practice dragon back at DSA."

"Turn your back on Straw Guts, Stickley," Coach was saying. "He's stalking. What do you do?"

"Run!" cried Stickley. He galloped across the castle yard.

"A big fat F for Stickley," Coach muttered, making a mark on his clipboard. "One of you new slackers try it. Zoomer?"

Angus trotted over and turned his back on the practice dragon slayer.

"Straw Guts is sneaking up on you," said Coach. "He's getting close. Now whirl around and give him a blast. Got it?"

Angus nodded. He spun toward the practice dragon slayer, and shot a huge ball of fire from his mouth. Old Straw Guts's head burst into flame.

"Oh, tail rot!" cried Coach Blazer. He blew

his whistle. "Douser, get on it!"

Douser bounced over to old Straw Guts and belched out a spray of water. The practice dragon slayer had lost most of his head, but otherwise wasn't damaged.

Coach turned to Angus. "It's a practice dragon slayer, you doofus!" he said. "You're supposed to use your practice flame! Don't you know anything?"

"Guess not," muttered Angus.

Coach Blazer looked suspicious. Next, he called on Wiglaf to do the Sword Whip.

"The sword what?" said Wiglaf.

"Oh, come on. Every dragon knows the sword whip by the time he leaves nursery school, Blinky." Coach made a note on his clipboard. "Sissy, show him how it's done."

"Who, me?" said Sissy. "Well, okay, guys, here I go."

She stepped up to old Straw Guts, spun around, and with a single, well-placed thrash of her tail, knocked the sword neatly out of the practice dragon slayer's hand.

Wiglaf was impressed.

After class ended, the three new dragons hoped to sneak off and try to summon Zelnoc again. But the hallways were mobbed, and every classroom was full.

"That was wicked cool, Zoomer," Taxi told Angus as they headed for Professor Scales's class, All About Dragon Slayers. "Using your real flame in class!"

When they reached the classroom, Angus said, "Let's get seats in the back row. Then maybe we won't get called on."

"But I like to sit in the front," said Erica. "I like to get called on."

"Not at *this* DSA you don't." Angus guided Erica to the back of the room.

Sissy, Stickley, Taxi, and Douser hurried to get seats near Angus. He was something of a hero now, after setting fire to old Straw Guts.

Most of the dragon students were still milling about when a tall, thin, pea-green dragon, who was more neck than body, walked through the door. He carried a briefcase.

"Seats, slackers," Professor Scales said. "Pass your homework papers up to me."

The dragon students shuffled papers in their notebooks. But no one found any homework.

"Slacking off again?" Professor Scales shook his head. Then he dug in his briefcase and pulled out a stack of papers. "I graded yesterday's test. You all failed. No surprise. Pay attention today and maybe some of you will pass the next test. That would make history, but it could happen. Okay. First question: Why do dragon slayers hunt dragons? Douser?"

"Uhhhh," said Douser. He scrunched up his face as if thinking very hard.

"Anyone?"

No claws went up.

Wiglaf glanced at Erica. He knew it was hard for her to keep from raising her claw.

"Dragon slayers slay dragons to take their gold and eat it," said Professor Scales.

Wiglaf, Angus, and Erica looked at one another, puzzled.

"Next question," said the professor. "What do dragon slayers wear in pouches around their necks?"

"Pouches around their necks?" whispered Angus. "What's he talking about?"

"Dragon slayers collect dragon teeth for good luck," Professor Scales answered himself. "They keep them in a little pouch."

Wiglaf couldn't believe his ears, which were now only small holes on the sides of his head.

"Third question," said Professor Scales. "Say a dragon slayer is coming after you. What's the best way to frighten him away? Taxi? Wild guess?"

The black-and-yellow dragon shrugged. "Say 'boo'?"

"Petunias," said Professor Scales. "One whiff of a petunia will knock a dragon slayer out cold."

"What?" cried Erica. She jumped to her feet.

Wiglaf and Angus tried to pull her back down, but they were too late.

"A slacker with a question," said the professor. "My, my. What is it?"

"Dragon slayers don't eat gold," Erica said. "They spend it."

Dragon students gasped. Wiglaf's crest started flashing. He wished Erica would stop.

"Dragon slayers don't collect dragon teeth," she said. "And no dragon slayer has ever fainted from smelling a petunia. Everything you said is wrong!"

"Oh, really?" Professor Scales smiled. Then he shouted, "Clear your desks! Pop quiz!"

"Oh, no!" cried all the dragon students.

"Don't blame me." Professor Scales began slapping test papers down on their desks. "Blame the dragon in the back row. She thinks she knows all about dragon slayers."

Several of the dragon students turned around in their seats and shot Erica dirty looks.

When Professor Scales got to the last row, he bent down close to Erica.

"There's something fishy about you, Silvershine," he said. His eyes darted to Angus and Wiglaf. "And your little slacker friends, too. I'm going to find out what it is."

"I told the truth," Erica whispered to her friends when class was finally over. "So what if Professor Scales didn't like it? We aren't going to be around here much longer. During lunch, when everyone's in the cafeteria, we'll summon Zelnoc. He'll get us out of here."

Next was Flaming Class. Buckets of water and fire extinguishers were everywhere in the classroom. Wiglaf took a seat between Angus and Erica.

"Velcome to Flaming Class!" said a swamp-green dragon with a burnt-orange horn atop his knobby head. "For you new slackers, I am Earl von Flambe, your instructor."

That name—von Flambe. Wiglaf had heard it before, but where?

"Flaming is a dragon's most vicked veapon," Earl von Flambe went on. "It's vhat dragons are known for. Vhy else vould folks call us 'fire-breathers'?"

Wiglaf nudged Erica. "I know that name from somewhere," he said. "Von Flambe."

"Sshhh!" said Erica. "I want to hear what he says about flaming."

"Before ve practice flaming," said Earl, "I vill get you all vorked up so your flames vill be vild and vonderful!" He grinned, showing a mouth full of mossy green teeth. "Vat vould you do if you met the vorld's vorst dragon slayer?"

"Run!" called Stickley.

"Beg for mercy," said Sissy.

"Hand over all my gold," said Taxi.

"Use your vits, slackers," Earl said. "Vhat vould you do if you met a really vicked dragon slayer? A dragon slayer who vanted to slay *you*?"

"Uh..." said Taxi. "Try to talk him out of it?"

"Vat are you saying?" said Earl. "You vould flame him! Bar-b-que him! Charcoal grill him! Ha! That vould vake him up!"

Wiglaf thought Earl seemed way over-excited about this assignment.

"Now, students," Earl went on, "vat is the name of this dragon slayer? The most vicked dragon slayer, the vorst one in the whole vorld?"

All together, the dragon students shouted out, "Wiglaf of Pinwick!"

Chapter 7

Wiglaf's crest flashed. He felt his blood turn cold. He had never been so scared.

Angus reached over and took one of Wiglaf's claws. Erica held the other.

What was Earl von Flambe talking about? Wiglaf wondered. How could he, Wiglaf of Pinwick, be the most wicked dragon slayer in the whole world?

And suddenly, it hit him.

"I know where I heard that name," he whispered. "Seetha! Seetha von Flambe!"

Seetha was a terrible dragon, and her son Gorzil was just as bad. Wiglaf had slain Gorzil—by accident, of course. Then Seetha came after Wiglaf, seeking revenge. He had spent a ghastly afternoon clutched in her claw. He shuddered, remembering how she'd dangled him high above the DSA castle moat. Wiglaf had drawn the dagger he'd hidden in his boot. But the thought of actually stabbing anyone—even Seetha—made him feel so sick that he'd dropped it. The dagger's tip had hit Seetha's toe, which caused her to fall into the moat, where she sank to the bottom. So Wiglaf had more or less slain Seetha, too.

"Seetha had lots of children," said Angus.

"Three-thousand six-hundred eighty-four," said Erica, who had a head for numbers.

"Earl must be one of them." Wiglaf swallowed. He stared at the angry dragon ranting on and on at the front of the class. Earl looked like Seetha. He had the same swamp-green scales. The same burnt-orange horn. Same yellow eyes. Same mossy green teeth.

"We'll summon Zelnoc," Erica whispered.

"Right after class," added Angus.

Wiglaf could tell that his friends were trying to appear calm. But they looked almost as frightened as he felt. Right now, however, there was nothing to do but sit and listen to Earl von Flambe.

"If I ever find this Viglaf, also known as Viggie, I vill vack off his head!" Earl was saying. "I vill vomp him! I vill vallop him! I vill put him on a spit and flambe him!"

Please, please don't let Zelnoc's dragon spell wear off now! Wiglaf chanted over and over while Earl showed his students how to hiss green sparks.

"Sssssssss o cool!" said Angus, producing a shower of sparks.

"Sssssssss sssuper!" said Erica, spitting sparks galore.

"Try it, Wiggie," said Erica.

"I'm too scared," said Wiglaf.

Suddenly, Earl von Flambe was standing next to Wiglaf's desk.

"Vhat are you vaiting for?" said Earl. "Vhere are your sparks?"

"Sssssssomewhere," Wiglaf hissed. But no green sparks appeared.

Earl von Flambe wrinkled his brow. "Vhat do you know," he mumbled. "A dragon that vill not spit sparks. Very vorrisome." He walked off, shaking his head.

"Buck up, Wiggie," said Erica. "We'll be out of here soon."

"The sooner the better," said Wiggie, sending a lone spark into the air.

At last, Earl von Flambe said, "I vill dismiss you now. Farevell!"

Wiglaf was the first dragon out the door.

"Come on," he said, when Erica and Angus straggled out the door. "We have to summon Zelnoc."

"Hey, Wiglaf? Oops, I mean, Blinky?" said Angus. "Let's stick around for one more class."

"What?" said Wiglaf. "No!"

"Come on, Wiggie," said Erica. "Please? It's Flying Class. Once Zelnoc changes us back, we won't be able to fly, ever again. It's our last chance."

Wiglaf sighed. "Oh, all right," he said. "I guess one more class won't make any difference."

Flying Class was held in the castle yard. Wiglaf spotted the teacher. He was slim and elegant, light green with silvery trim—crest, claws, back fins. A pair of goggles sat atop his head.

"Hi, Ace!" said Sissy as she ran toward him. "Did you meet the new guys? That's Silvershine, Zoomer, and Blinky."

"Ace Lizzard here," said the teacher. "Ready to do some fancy flying?"

"Ready!" said Angus.

Ace grinned. "Let me see your stuff, daredevil."

Angus spread his wings and took off. He

circled once overhead and circled again. He wobbled a bit, dropping several feet. But he managed to catch himself and land.

"How was I?" asked Angus, panting to catch his breath.

"Good," said Ace. "For pre-kindergarten. You call yourself a dragon?"

Angus's face fell.

"Sissy," Ace was saying, "show him your stuff."

"Aw, no, Ace," whined Sissy. "Don't make me show off. These guys are behind in everything. They must have gone to a really bad school. But it's not their fault."

"Sissy..." said Ace again.

Sissy sighed. Wiglaf and the others watched as she spread her wings and took to the skies. She did a quadruple somersault loop-the-loop triple lutz with a half-twist jackknife backflip double-axel skydive. Then she did some really hard stuff. She landed lightly on her hind legs.

"Awesome!" breathed Erica.

"Students, do some sprints to warm up for the fifty-yard sky dash," Ace said. "I want a word with the new students."

Wiglaf's crest began blinking in alarm. Did Ace suspect that they weren't real dragons?

But Ace's attention had turned to the castle. Madam Dragonova was lumbering down the steps to the yard. Drigon lurched at her side, as did a large orange dragon. This one was carrying lots of lumpy packs. Behind them, dragon students and teachers poured out the castle door.

"Mr. Lizzard!" Madam Dragonova called to the flying teacher. "Classes are cancelled for the rest of the morning. We've got a situation!"

Wiglaf's heart was thumping in time with his flashing crest. Had they been found out?

Madam Dragonova pointed to Wiglaf, Angus, and Erica. "New slackers, up against the castle wall, pronto!" she shouted.

Wiglaf felt dizzy with fear as he, Erica, and Angus backed up against the high stone wall. Was the big orange dragon an executioner? Were they about to be offed by dragon firing squad?

"They know!" Wiglaf whispered.

"We're doomed!" whimpered Angus.

"Wiggie!" said Erica. "Call Zelnoc!"

Chapter 8

iglaf started chanting: "Conlez! Con—"

"Blinker!" shouted Madam Dragonova. "Shut your trap!"

Wiglaf stopped mid-chant.

"The rest of you, line up over there!" Madam Dragonova pointed and waved. "Go on! Shortest in the front. Tall ones next. Teachers, in the back row. You know the drill."

What was going on? The entire school was now standing with their backs to the wall.

"This is Mr. Sketcher," Madam Dragonova said, with a nod toward the orange dragon. "He got confused and came a day early for School Picture Day, but we're just going with it."

Relief flooded through Wiglaf. It was only a

group shot for School Picture Day!

"Mr. Sketcher draws fast," Madam went on. "But you'll have to hold still or you won't be in the picture. Say moat weed!" She sat down in a throne-like chair in the center of the group.

The three brand-new dragons stood still and smiled with the rest of DSA. At last, Mr. Sketcher looked up from his drawing pad and said, "Done!"

"Thank you, Mr. Sketcher," Madam Dragonova said, rising. "Those of you whose parents bought the package with individual pictures, stay here. The rest of you, go to lunch."

"Oh, boy!" Angus raced into the castle, with Erica and Wiglaf right behind.

When they reached the cafeteria, they discovered they were the only three who hadn't stayed for individual pictures.

"That was a close one," said Angus, sitting down at the Class I table. "I thought they figured out that we're faking it."

"I thought so, too, for a minute," said Erica, reaching for the pepper. "But why would they? We do everything the other dragons do. We totally fit in."

Wiglaf made himself shovel in a mouthful of slimy weedghetti. All at once, he got a funny feeling that he was being watched. He looked up and nearly choked. Towering over their table were Madam Dragonova, Coach Blazer, Professor Scales, Earl von Flambe, and Ace Lizzard. The huge scaly teachers glared down at them.

Wiglaf's flashing crest made Angus and Erica look up, too.

"Uh-oh," said Angus.

"I've just heard some interesting reports from your teachers, slackers," Madam said. "Zoomer, Coach Blazer says you nearly burned up old Straw Guts. Blinky, I hear you don't know the Sword Whip."

"Our old school was awful," Angus said, shaking his head. "We never learned a thing."

"Vhat school vas that?" asked Earl.

"Uh...Dragon School Academy," said Angus. "Very small. Not up to speed."

Wiglaf admired the way Angus was handling himself. But how long could he keep going before he tripped up?

"That one—" Professor Scales pointed a claw at Erica. "—is a troublemaker."

"Vhat's his name," said Earl, pointing at Wiglaf, "vasn't hissing sparks. There is something very veird about him."

"And Zoomer there flies like a two-year-old," added Ace.

Madam Dragonova's plum-colored eyes bulged angrily. "You're not real dragons," she said. "You're impostors!"

"What?" said Angus. "No, we're dragons. Look, scales. Horns. Sharp teeth." He grinned.

"Ve vill see," said Earl. "Ve vill give you the Real Dragon Test."

Wiglaf's crest began flashing at hyper speed.

"Say the last line of this rhyme that every pipling dragon knows," said Professor Scales.

> *"Mary Dragon had a lamb,*
> *Had a lamb, had a lamb,*
> *Mary Dragon had a lamb..."*

The dragon teachers waited.

Wiglaf shrugged. Erica looked panic-stricken.

Angus took a guess. "Its fleece was white as snow?"

"No!" boomed Professor Scales. " 'For breakfast, lunch, and dinner!' "

Wiglaf swallowed. How could they ever pass this test?

"Vell, vell, vell," said Earl. "Try this one:

> *Tvinkle, tvinkle, vee small star,*

Dragons vonder vhat you are.

Up above the vorld so dark..."

This time, Angus shrugged. So did Erica.

Wiglaf gave it a try: "Like a diamond in the...park?"

"Vhat?" cried Earl. "No! It's 'Like a vee small dragon spark!' " Earl brought his face down close to Wiglaf's. "Who are you?" he asked.

"Call Zelnoc, Wiggie!" cried Erica. She clapped her claws over her mouth. "I mean, Blinky."

"Viggie?" Earl's yellow eyes grew wide. "Viggie, short for Viglaf?" He grabbed Wiglaf's front leg and began to squeeze. "Are you Viglaf of Pinvick?"

"It must be magic! They are not dragons—they're dragon slayers!" shouted Madam Dragonova.

"Yow!" Wiglaf yelped as Earl's claws dug into his flesh.

"I've vaited and vaited for this moment!" cried Earl. "Ever since you slew my vonderful mother, Seetha!"

"I never meant to!" cried Wiglaf.

"You vacked my brother, too!" said Earl.

"Another accident!" cried Wiglaf. "I swear!"

Earl kept squeezing. "This Zelnoc," he said. "Is he a vizard?"

Wiglaf nodded again.

"So the vizard did a spell and von, two, three, you turned into dragons?" asked Earl.

Wiglaf was getting sick of nodding.

"I knew something was wrong with them!" exclaimed Madam Dragonova.

Earl was beaming. "Vait until my brothers and sisters hear that Viglaf of Pinvick, the vorld's vorst dragon slayer, is a prisoner at DSA!" he cried. "I'm going to call them—all 3,682 of them! Oh, vhat fun ve'll have vhen they get here."

Chapter 9

The DSA dungeon was hot. It reeked of rot and mildew. It had one tiny barred window way up high. Wiglaf saw a spider the size of a dinner plate climbing up the wall.

Iron cuffs cut into Wiglaf's legs. Even worse was the gag tied tightly across his mouth. If he could only get a piece of it between his teeth! Maybe he could gnaw it off.

Erica and Angus were chained to the opposite wall of the cell. Erica kept grunting through her gag. Wiglaf figured she was saying she was sorry for blurting out his name. He was sorry, too. Very sorry! Who knew what awful things Seetha's 3,683 children would do?

There! He'd gotten the gag to slip. He started gnawing. SNAP! The gag fell to the floor.

Wiglaf limbered up his lips. Then he quickly chanted: "Conlez! Conlez! Conlez!"

A tiny cloud of blue smoke appeared. It grew until it filled the dungeon. Wiglaf could hardly breathe. He saw Zelnoc's shape inside the smoke. The wizard took off his pointed hat, held it upside-down, and said, "Vacuum!" The smoke quickly poured itself into the hat and vanished.

The wizard's eyes widened at the sight of the three dragons chained to the dungeon wall.

"Am I summoned by dragons?" he cried.

"It's me, Wiglaf. You messed up your wing spell, remember?"

"Ah, Wagloof!" said Zelnoc. "It's all coming back to me now."

Wiglaf rattled his chains. "Can you get us out of here and turn us back into our old selves?" he said. "And fast! There are 3,683 angry dragons on their way here to get me."

"That many?" Zelnoc tapped his fingers on his chin, thinking. "I've got it. First, I'll get you out of your chains." Zelnoc pulled his wand from his sleeve and began to chant:

"Wave my wand!"

The wizard waved his wand at each dragon in turn.

"And cross my eyes!"

Zelnoc faced each of them with his eyes aimed straight for the tip of his nose.

"All before me—minimize!"

Wiglaf felt dizzy, as he always did when Zelnoc put a spell on him. Then he felt the chains slipping off. Zelnoc stopped chanting. Wiglaf looked around the dungeon. He'd never noticed how truly huge it was. Where was the wizard? And why were there two enormous shoes in the middle of the floor?

"Wagloop?" a voice boomed from above.

Way above. Wiglaf looked up and saw the wizard towering above him like a mountain.

"Wiggie!" a silver scaled dragon scampered over to him. "Zelnoc's shrunk us!"

The blue dragon was right behind her. "We're no bigger than lizards!"

"Zelnoc!" cried Wiglaf. "Not again!"

"What?" boomed the wizard. "Are you suggesting that my spell went haywire? No such thing. That's just what I meant to do. The chain-snapping spell is far more complicated. You'd still be prisoners if I'd gone that route. And that would be bad for you. Because I hear footsteps in the hallway. I'm out of here, Wuglop. Good luck!"

With a bright flash of light, the wizard was gone.

Now, Wiglaf heard the pounding of feet. Many feet. An army of dragons! The sound grew closer and closer.

The tiny dragons stared at one another,

frozen with fear. They heard dragons growling.

"There's a rat hole!" Wiglaf squeaked. "Quick!"

The three dashed into the hole in the wall. In the nick of time, too. Angus had just pulled his tail inside the musty cavern when the dungeon door creaked open.

"Vhat?" cried Earl. "Vhy, they've vanished!"

Wiglaf clung to Angus and Erica. All he could see from inside the rat hole were dozens of dragon feet. He heard Drigon grunting.

"I vonder if they summoned that vizard?" said Earl. "Anyvay, they can't have gone far. Ve vill find them, no matter vhat!"

Wiglaf listened as the sound of pounding dragon feet faded into the distance. Then he let out a long breath. He'd managed to squeak by another encounter with Earl. But he knew there'd be a next time.

"Aaaah!" Angus shrieked and he darted out of the rat hole.

Wiglaf whirled around and saw three big rats standing behind them.

"We can take them!" Erica shouted.

"Aw, hey, no," said the biggest rat. "We don't want to fight."

"Oh, good," said Wiglaf. "We don't, either."

"Got any crumbs?" asked the second-biggest rat.

"Sorry," said Wiglaf. "Listen, we have to get out of here. So, thanks for the hiding place."

"No problem," said the smallest rat. "Good luck!"

"The window!" cried Erica. "We're small enough to fly through the bars."

Wiglaf and the other tiny dragons spread their wings and flapped up and out of the dungeon window. They hovered there for a moment, getting their bearings.

"Let's fly back to our DSA," said Angus.

"But we're so small," said Erica. "It'll take forever."

"Look out!" cried Wiglaf as Sissy zoomed by, nearly crashing into the three tiny dragons.

"Whoa!" she called, veering at the last moment to avoid hitting them. She flapped her wings slowly, treading air. "Hey, guys! You're, like, so small!"

"I know," said Wiglaf. "Listen, Sissy—"

But Sissy wasn't listening. She was yelling down to the other dragons in Flying Class. "Hey, guys!" she shouted. "Look! Here's Zoomer and Silvershine and Blinky!"

"Sissy, no!" cried Wiglaf.

But all the dragons on the ground had heard, including Ace Lizzard.

"Grab them, Sissy!" called Ace. "They're not really dragons. They're dragon *slayers* in disguise!"

"Oh, Mr. Lizzard, you gotta be joking," said Sissy.

"No joke!" said Ace. "They'll slay you if

they get the chance. We took them prisoner, but they escaped from the dungeon. Come on, class. Let's go get them!" He spread an enormous pair of wings and took off. The students in the class flew after him.

"Wow!" said Sissy as she took to the air. "I was totally fooled."

The three tiny dragons zoomed and darted through the air, terrified. Ace and every dragon in his class zoomed after them. Wiglaf lost track of Angus and Erica. His flying muscles hurt. He was getting tired. How much longer could he keep this up?

Wiglaf knew his blinking crest was like a sign that said, "Come and get me!" He had to land. He had to hide. But where?

Suddenly, claws seemed to come out of nowhere. They closed around him. He was caught! There was nothing he could do. He, Wiglaf of Pinwick, was a goner.

The dragon landed. It loosened its grip.

Wiglaf started breathing again. He looked up at his captor.

"Sissy!" he squeaked.

"Yeah," said Sissy. "It's me. I trusted you guys!"

Wiglaf saw Erica and Angus in her other claw.

"Don't turn us in, Sissy," begged Wiglaf. "We *are* dragon slayers. But we don't want to kill any dragons...you're our friends."

"For sure?" Sissy sounded doubtful.

"For sure!" Wiglaf, Erica, and Angus all cried.

"Well...friends are friends, no matter what. Stay here in the henhouse, guys."

Sissy put them on a high wooden rafter beneath one of the many holes in the henhouse roof. "I'll be back to get you."

"Thanks, Sissy!" called Wiglaf and the others as she darted out the door.

"I'll summon Zelnoc," said Wiglaf.

"Fugettaboutit," said Erica. "I'm going straight to the top. The head wizard, Zizmor. That's who we need." And she began chanting his name backwards, "ROMZIZ! ROMZIZ! ROMZIZ!"

Chapter 10

 tornado of red smoke appeared inside the henhouse. The hens clucked wildly and ran out the door. The three tiny dragons flew down from their perch, eager to greet the Amazing One, the most powerful of all wizards.

From out of the whirling red smoke stepped—a baby! He had on a red wizard's robe and hat that were way too big for him. He was sucking his thumb.

Wiglaf gasped. "Zizmor?" he said. "Is that you?"

"Gaaaa!" cried the baby, catching sight of the little dragons. He ran after them. He

scooped up Wiglaf in his pudgy hand and began to squeeze.

"Stop!" Wiglaf cried. "I can't breathe!" Had he escaped death by 3,683 dragons only to be crushed by a baby?

"Let go, baby!" cried Erica.

"No!" cried baby Ziz gleefully. "No! No! No!"

Suddenly, a column of blue smoke appeared. Out of it stepped Zelnoc.

"Warts and moles!" he cried. "What timing! I was just getting ready to do the spell-reversal spell on Ziz when you summoned him." The wizard drew a big red lollipop from the pocket of his robe and held it out to Zizmor. The baby grabbed for the candy, dropping Wiglaf.

Wiglaf shook out his wings and straightened his crest. "Can you do the spell on all of us, Zelnoc?" he asked. "We're in big trouble here."

"Why not?" said the wizard. "Stand next to Ziz. I'll do you all in a batch."

The dragons scurried over to stand next to baby Ziz.

Zelnoc extended gnarly fingers in their direction and began to chant:

"As you were before my spell, so shall you be again,

When I finish counting down from the number ten.

Ten!

Nine!"

Wiglaf felt the dizziness overtake him.

"Eight!

Seven!

Six!"

He felt his body growing, changing shape.

"Five!

Four!

Three!

Two!

One!"

Wiglaf felt a jolt. He looked down. He had

arms. Hands. Legs. Feet. He was a boy again. Angus and Erica were back to normal, too. Beside them stood an ancient, tall, white-bearded Zizmor.

"Ah, I'm me again!" cried Zizmor. He slapped the lesser wizard on the back. "Zelnoc, at the next Wizards' Convention, I want you to—"

"Give a speech, Ziz?" said Zelnoc eagerly. "Tell how I did a spell-reversal spell?"

"Be in charge of cleanup," said Zizmor. "And any other nasty jobs I can think of!"

Zelnoc's face fell. "Yes, Amazing One," he muttered. "Whatever you say."

"I say we shove off," said Zizmor. "Ready, Zelnoc?"

"Ready, Chief," said Zelnoc.

"Wait!" cried Wiglaf. "Hold it! You have to get us out of here!"

But he found himself shouting into thick red and blue smoke. The wizards had vanished.

Through the fading smoke, Wiglaf saw a slice of light. The henhouse doors creaked open and in ran Sissy.

"Okay, guys, here's the plan," she whispered.

But before she could say another word, Madam Dragonova rushed in. She eyed Wiglaf, Erica, and Angus. "Puny little things, aren't you?" she said.

Behind her, through the open doorway, Wiglaf saw that the DSA castle yard was filled with thousands of dragons. Seetha's children!

Madam kicked the door shut. She eyed the three small dragon slayers-in-training. "Dragon slayers steal hoards of dragon gold," she said, keeping her voice low. "Tell me where yours is. And quick! Before those ruffians out there break down the door to get you."

"We—we don't have it on us," said Wiglaf, eager to talk or do anything to keep from going out to the castle yard. "But before a wizard's spell changed us into dragons, we were on our way to Hermit Harry's Hut. We're supposed to fetch our headmaster a Jiffy-Gold."

"Jiffy what?" said Madam.

"It's an alchemy kit," added Erica.

"Turns common household items to gold," said Angus.

Madam Dragonova's scaly eyebrows went up. "To gold?"

Wiglaf nodded. "You can get a Jiffy-Gold kit free, this week only."

"It's a special offer," said Angus.

"After a week, if you aren't satisfied," Erica said, "you can return it, no questions asked."

Madam Dragonova looked thoughtful. "I wouldn't mind having one of those kits myself."

"We can get you one," Wiglaf offered.

"Really?" Madam's eyes lit up.

"We'll set off right now," offered Wiglaf.

"Sissy," said Madam. "Give them a ride to the hermit's hut. And hurry! Before the offer expires. Go on! Why, just think, in a week, I can Jiffy-Gold this whole castle!"

Wiglaf, Erica, and Angus straddled Sissy's back. They held on tight as she winged over mountaintops. Wiglaf thought he liked riding a dragon better than he liked being one.

On they flew, until Angus said, "What stinks?"

Wiglaf looked down. Way below them was a little hovel with a long line of people outside.

"It's Harry's," he said.

The dragon came in for a landing.

"You know, guys, I can't go get a kit myself," said Sissy. "Everyone would panic and run away."

Sissy waited on the edge of Nowhere Swamp while Wiglaf, Angus, and Erica stood in line. The closer they got to Harry's, the worse it smelled.

At last, it was their turn to stand before the dirty tangled-haired hermit.

"What'll it be?" asked Harry. He nearly knocked them off their feet with his breath.

"Two Jiffy-Gold kits, please," Wiglaf managed.

"Here's one," said Harry. Angus carried the box to Sissy while Wiglaf and Angus waited for Harry to bring back another. But just as he was handing it to them, a gong sounded.

"Ah, time's up!" said Harry. "The Special Offer has expired."

A loud wail went up from everyone still standing in line.

"You can still get a kit!" Harry yelled over the wails. "You just have to pay for it."

"Mordred wants a kit," said Wiglaf. "But he won't want to pay for it."

"Oh, he can pay for it out of the gold he makes," said Erica. "We'll take it," she told Harry.

Wiglaf and Erica walked over to the edge of the swamp. Angus had managed to strap

Madam's Jiffy-Gold kit to Sissy's back.

"So long, guys!" said Sissy. "Will you come back and see us someday?"

"It would be very dangerous," Wiglaf pointed out. "Earl is out to get me."

"Hey, maybe Taxi and Stickley and I can come visit you guys!" said Sissy.

"That could be dangerous for you," said Wiglaf. "Our DSA is Dragon Slayers' Academy."

"Okay, guys," said Sissy. "Guess I'll see you when I see you!" She waved, then rose up into the air. Wiglaf, Angus, and Erica watched her until she disappeared from view.

"Rats!" said Angus. "We should have gotten her to give us a lift back to school."

Erica groaned. "Why didn't we think of that? Now we have to walk."

Wiglaf picked up the kit. It was surprisingly light. "Off we go," he said.

Night fell as they trudged through the Dark

Forest. The three walked all night. At daybreak, they reached their DSA. Wiglaf was tired and hungry and, oh, so glad to be back.

How small the castle yard looked! When they reached Mordred's office, Angus knocked on the door. "Uncle Mordred!" he called. "Here's the Jiffy-Gold kit!"

The door swung open. "What took you so long?" the headmaster growled. He grabbed the box from his nephew's hands and tore open the lid.

Wiglaf had been curious to see what a Jiffy-Gold kit looked like. He watched as Mordred lifted a large tube and a pouch from the box.

"*This* is the Jiffy-Gold?" cried Mordred.

Wiglaf saw that the tube was labeled *GLUE*. And the pouch, *GLITTER*. Mordred loosened the pouch strings and poured a few sparkles into his hand.

"This isn't an alchemy kit!" Mordred yelled. "It's worthless humbug! And what's this?" He pulled out a piece of parchment from the box. "Why, it's a *bill*!" His eyes bulged scarily as he read it. "It says I owe Harry three pieces of gold, and if he doesn't get it by the end of the week, he'll set his pack of hounds on me!"

Mordred glared at the three dragon slayers-in-training.

"You three will work off that gold!" he shouted. "Get to the kitchen. On the double! There's a mountain of pots waiting to be scrubbed. Go, go, GO!"

Wiglaf, Erica, and Angus turned and ran from the headmaster's office.

"At least we're just in time for breakfast," said Angus. "I bet I'll get there first!"

"Not a chance," said Erica, breaking into a run.

Wiglaf put on a burst of speed. For the first time ever, he couldn't wait to take a bite of Frypot's scrambled eel.

Mordred de Marvelous

Mordred graduated from Dragon Bludgeon High, second in his class. The other student, Lionel Flyzwattar, went on to become headmaster of Dragon Stabbers' Prep. Mordred spent years as part-time, semi-substitute student teacher at Dragon Whackers' Alternative School, all the while pursuing his passion for mud wrestling. Inspired by how filthy rich Flyzwattar had become by running a school, Mordred founded Dragon Slayers' Academy in CMLXXIV, and has served as headmaster ever since.

⚜

Known to the Boys as: Mordred de Miser
Dream: Piles and piles of dragon gold
Reality: Yet to see a single gold coin
Best-Kept Secret: Mud wrestled under the name Macho-Man Mordie
Plans for the Future: Will retire to the Bahamas . . . as soon as he gets his hands on a hoard

Lady Lobelia

Lobelia de Marvelous is Mordred's sister and a graduate of the exclusive If-You-Can-Read-This-You-Can-Design-Clothes Fashion School. Lobelia has offered fashion advice to the likes of King Felix the Husky and Eric the Terrible Dresser. In CMLXXIX, Lobelia married the oldest living knight, Sir Jeffrey Scabpicker III. That's when she gained the title of Lady Lobelia, but—alas!—only a very small fortune, which she wiped out in a single wild shopping spree. Lady Lobelia has graced Dragon Slayers' Academy with many visits, and can be heard around campus saying, "Just because I live in the Middle Ages doesn't mean I have to look middle-aged."

❧

Known to the Boys as: Lady Lo Lo
Dream: Frightfully fashionable
Reality: Frightful
Best-Kept Secret: Shops at Dark-Age Discount Dress Dungeon
Plans for the Future: New uniforms for the boys with mesh tights and lace tunics

Sir Mort du Mort

Sir Mort is our well-loved professor of Dragon Slaying for Beginners as well as Intermediate and Advanced Dragon Slaying. Sir Mort says that, in his youth, he was known as the Scourge of Dragons. (We're not sure what it means, but it sounds scary.) His last encounter was with the most dangerous dragon of them all: Knight-shredder. Early in the battle, Sir Mort took a nasty blow to his helmet and has never been the same since.

✦

Known to the Boys as: The Old Geezer
Dream: Outstanding Dragon Slayer
Reality: Just plain out of it
Best-Kept Secret: He can't remember
Plans for the Future: Taking a little nap

Coach Wendell Plungett

Coach Plungett spent many years questing in the Dark Forest before joining the Athletic Department at DSA. When at last he strode out of the forest, leaving his dragon-slaying days behind him, Coach Plungett was the most muscle-bulging, physically fit, manliest man to be found anywhere north of Nowhere Swamp. "I am what you call a hunk," the coach admits. At DSA, Plungett wears a number of hats—or, helmets. Besides PE Teacher, he is Slaying Coach, Square-Dance Director, Pep-Squad Sponsor, and Privy Inspector. He hopes to meet a damsel—she needn't be in distress—with whom he can share his love of heavy metal music and long dinners by candlelight.

❧

Known to the Boys as: Coach
Dream: Tough as nails
Reality: Sleeps with a stuffed dragon named Foofoo
Best-Kept Secret: Just pull his hair
Plans for the Future: Finding his lost lady love

Brother Dave

Brother Dave is the DSA librarian. He belongs to the Little Brothers of the Peanut Brittle, an order known for doing impossibly good deeds and cooking up endless batches of sweet peanut candy. How exactly did Brother Dave wind up at Dragon Slayers' Academy? After a batch of his extra-crunchy peanut brittle left three children from Toenail toothless, Brother Dave vowed to do a truly impossible good deed. Thus did he offer to be librarian at a school world-famous for considering reading and writing a complete and utter waste of time. Brother Dave hopes to change all that.

✤

Known to the Boys as: Bro Dave
Dream: Boys reading in the libary
Reality: Boys sleeping in the library
Best-Kept Secret: Uses Cliff's Notes
Plans for the Future: Copying out all the lyrics to "Found a Peanut" for the boys

~ Faculty ~

Professor Prissius Pluck

Professor Pluck graduated from Peter Piper Picked a Peck of Pickled Peppers Prep, and went on to become a professor of Science at Dragon Slayers' Academy. His specialty is the Multiple Choice Pop Test. The boys who take Dragon Science, Professor Pluck's popular class,

a) are amazed at the great quantities of saliva Professor P. can project

b) try never to sit in the front row

c) beg Headmaster Mordred to transfer them to another class

d) all of the above

⚜

Known to the Boys as: Old Spit Face
Dream: Proper pronunciation of *p*'s
Reality: Let us spray
Best-Kept Secret: Has never seen a pippi-hippo-pappa-peepus up close
Plans for the Future: Is working on a cure for chapped lips

Frypot

How Frypot came to be the cook at DSA is something of a mystery. Rumors abound. Some say that when Mordred bought the broken-down castle for his school, Frypot was already in the kitchen and he simply stayed on. Others say that Lady Lobelia hired Frypot because he was so speedy at washing dishes. Still others say Frypot knows many a dark secret that keeps him from losing his job. But no one ever, *ever* says that Frypot was hired because of his excellent cooking skills.

❧

Known to the Boys as: Who needs a nickname with a real name like Frypot?

Dream: Cleaner kitchen

Reality: Kitchen cleaner

Best-Kept Secret: Takes long bubble baths in the moat

Plans for the Future: Has signed up for a beginning cooking class

~ Staff ~

Yorick

Yorick is Chief Scout at DSA. His knack for masquerading as almost anything comes from his years with the Merry Minstrels and Dancing Damsels Players, where he won an award for his role as the Glass Slipper in *Cinderella*. However, when he was passed over for the part of Mama Bear in *Goldilocks*, Yorick decided to seek a new way of life. He snuck off in the night and, by dawn, still dressed in the bear suit, found himself walking up Huntsmans Path. Mordred spied him from a castle window, recognized his talent for disguise, and hired him as Chief Scout on the spot.

✤

Known to the Boys as: Who's that?
Dream: Master of Disguise
Reality: Mordred's Errand Boy
Best-Kept Secret: Likes dressing up as King Ken
Plans for the Future: To lose the bunny suit

Wiglaf of Pinwick

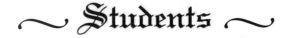

Wiglaf, our newest lad, hails from a hovel outside the village of Pinwick, which makes Toenail look like a thriving metropolis. Being one of thirteen children, Wiglaf had a taste of dorm life before coming to DSA and he fit right in. He started the year off with a bang when he took a stab at Coach Plungett's brown pageboy wig. Way to go, Wiggie! We hope to see more of this lad's wacky humor in the years to come.

⚜

Dream: Bold Dragon-Slaying Hero
Reality: Still hangs on to a "security" rag
Extracurricular Activities: Animal-Lovers Club, President; No More Eel for Lunch Club, President; Frypot's Scrub Team, Brush Wielder; Pig Appreciation Club, Founder
Favorite Subject: Library
Oft-Heard Saying: *"Ello-hay, Aisy-day!"*
Plans for the Future: To go for the gold!

~ Students ~

Angus du Pangus

The nephew of Mordred and
Lady Lobelia, Angus walks
the line between saying, "I'm
just one of the lads" and
"I'm going to tell my
uncle!" Will this Class I
lad ever become a mighty
dragon slayer? Or will he
take over the kitchen from
Frypot some day? We of
the DSA Yearbook staff are
betting on choice #2. And
hey, Angus? The sooner the
better!

Dream: A wider menu selection at DSA
Reality: Eel, Eel, Eel!
Extracurricular Activities: DSA Cooking Club,
President; Smilin' Hal's Off-Campus Eatery, Sales
Representative
Favorite Subject: Lunch
Oft-Heard Saying: *"I'm still hungry"*
Plans for the Future: To write *101 Ways to Cook a
Dragon*

Eric von Royale

Eric hails from Someplace Far Away (at least that's what he wrote on his Application Form). There's an air of mystery about this Class I lad, who says he is "totally typical and absolutely average." If that is so, how did he come to own the rich tapestry that hangs over his cot? And are his parents really close personal friends of Sir Lancelot? Did Frypot the cook bribe him to start the Clean Plate Club? And doesn't Eric's arm ever get tired from raising his hand in class so often?

⚜

Dream: Valiant Dragon Slayer
Reality: Teacher's Pet
Extracurricular Activities: Sir Lancelot Fan Club; Armor Polishing Club; Future Dragon Slayer of the Month Club; DSA Pep Squad, Founder and Cheer Composer
Favorite Subject: All of Them!!!!!
Oft-Heard Saying: *"When I am a mighty Dragon Slayer . . ."*
Plans for the Future: To take over DSA

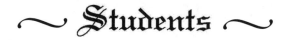

Baldrick de Bold

This is a banner year for Baldrick. He is celebrating his tenth year as a Class I lad at DSA. Way to go, Baldrick! If any of you new students want to know the ropes, Baldrick is the one to see. He can tell when you should definitely *not* eat the cafeteria's eel, where the choice seats are in Professor Pluck's class, and what to tell the headmaster if you are late to class. Just don't ask him the answer to any test questions.

❖

Dream: To run the world
Reality: A runny nose
Extracurricular Activities: Practice Dragon Maintenance Squad; Least Improved Slayer-in-Training Award
Favorite Subject: *"Could you repeat the question?"*
Oft Heard Saying: *"A dragon ate my homework."*
Plans for the Future: To transfer to Dragon Stabbers' Prep